Everything
but the
Horse

To my brothers,
Gary & Guy

Little, Brown and Company • Hachette Book Group • 237 Park Avenue, New York, NY 10017 • Visit our website at www.lb-kids.com

Little, Brown and Company is a division of Hachette Book Group, Inc.
The Little, Brown name and logo are trademarks of Hachette Book Group, Inc.

First Edition: October 2010

Library of Congress Cataloging-in-Publication Data

Hobbie, Holly.
Everything but the horse / Holly Hobbie. — 1st ed.
p. cm.
Summary: When Holly's family moves from the city to a farm, she longs to get a
horse for her birthday. Based on events in the author's childhood.
ISBN 978-0-316-07019-5
[1. Farm life—Fiction. 2. Country life—Fiction. 3. Horses—Fiction.
4. Hobbie, Holly—Childhood and youth—Fiction.] I. Title.
PZ7.H6517Ev 2010
[E] —dc22

2010006907

10 9 8 7 6 5 4 3 2 1

SC • Printed in China

The illustrations for this book were done in transparent watercolor and pen and ink.
The text was set in Zapf International, and the display type was set in Americana with hand lettering by Leah Palmer Preiss.

Everything but the Horse

A CHILDHOOD MEMORY BY

HOLLY HOBBIE

Little, Brown and Company
New York Boston

This is Sunnyside Avenue, and that's my grandfather's house. We lived on the third floor. That's my mother in the window, calling for me to come in.

Our neighborhood was packed with kids and cats and dogs and every sort of grown-up. We raced through yards and climbed over walls and fences, filling the air with shouts and laughter. It was the whole world to me, and I was right at home in it.

Then, clear out of the blue, my parents bought an old farm
on Middlebury Road. They planned to fix it up and make it our
own place in the country.

Plenty of stuff on a ramshackle farm can seem scary at first.

There was a tumbledown chicken coop guarded by a fierce rooster. Wild, unpettable cats slithered through the bushes. My bedroom upstairs was spooky because there was no electricity to light it up. And we had an outhouse for the toilet. That was so creepy I preferred to use the great outdoors.

Pretty soon, though, I fell in love with the woods and fields, with wildflowers and birds and country smells. And the biggest excitement of my new life, the best part, was raising animals.

There was Buster, our dog, and our own bunch of cats, but we also had ducks, ornery geese, and a coop full of chickens. My job was to talk softly to them while I collected their eggs. We had a pig for a while, my mother's gentle Clark, and a beautiful Guernsey cow named Tinkerbell, who followed me around the yard. I learned to milk her.

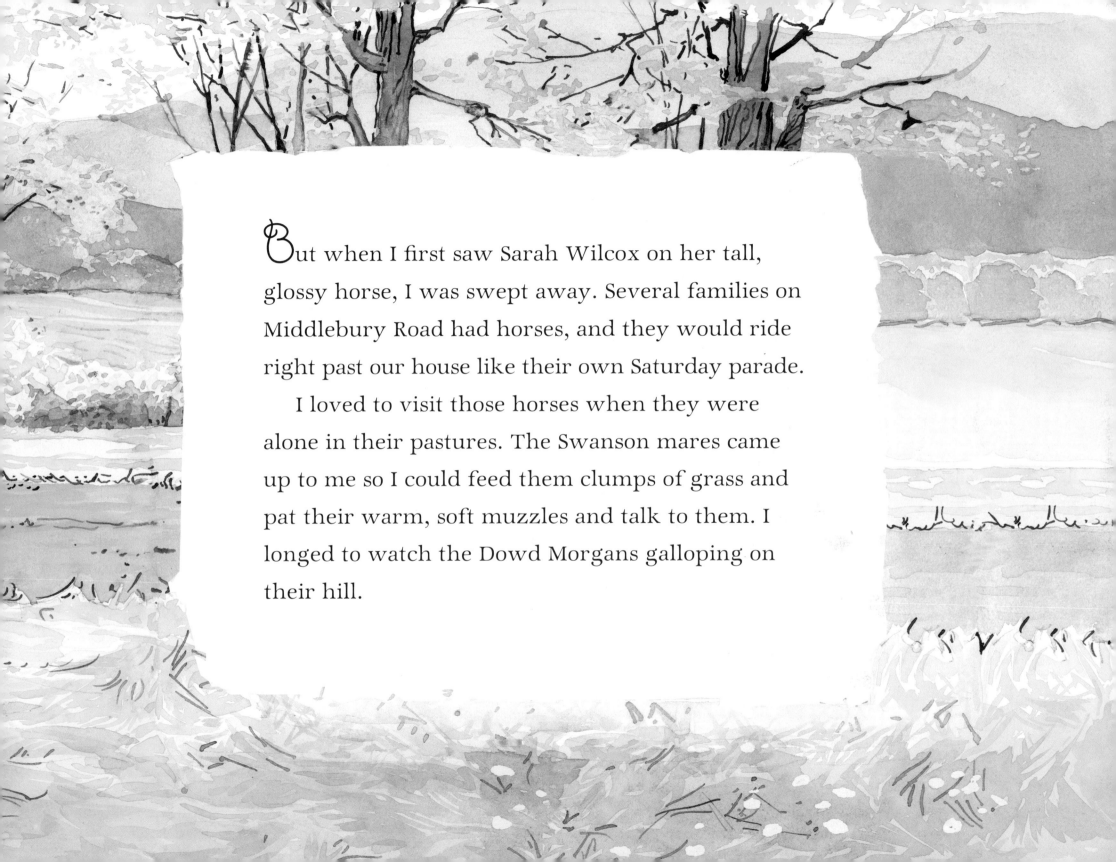

But when I first saw Sarah Wilcox on her tall, glossy horse, I was swept away. Several families on Middlebury Road had horses, and they would ride right past our house like their own Saturday parade.

I loved to visit those horses when they were alone in their pastures. The Swanson mares came up to me so I could feed them clumps of grass and pat their warm, soft muzzles and talk to them. I longed to watch the Dowd Morgans galloping on their hill.

Sarah Wilcox, who was in high school, usually waved to me as she rode her horse along her stone wall. The whole beautiful scene was like a movie. I could see myself riding beside her.

Well, we already had a pasture, for one thing. We had a barn with two stalls, which was perfect. The loft of the barn was full of sweet-smelling hay, and there were even bridles and harnesses hanging against one wall. We had everything anybody needed to have a horse, and a horse was the one and only thing I wanted more than anything in the world.

My grandmother said a horse was too dangerous. My father said a horse was too much trouble. My mother said we couldn't afford a horse. And my brothers said, "What do you need a horse for?"

I still wore my cowboy shirt all the time anyway.

Too dangerous!

Too much trouble!

Too much money!

Why? What for?

I collected horse droppings, which Mom called road apples, whenever the Swansons and the Dowds rode by our house, and I scattered them around the first stall in the barn, which made it seem like a horse lived there.

I took out library books that had pictures of horses and taught myself to draw them. I was already the best artist in the family and in my class at school, and my best pictures so far were my horse pictures. I plastered them all over the walls of my room.

I was proudest of my full-color painting of a black stallion.

Mom taped it over the fireplace in the living room.

"Aren't horses beautiful?" I asked her.

"Very beautiful," Mom said.

"Did you ever want one?"

"Oh, I must have," she said, "when I was your age."

Then it was my birthday. It was a beautiful day, and it was Halloween, too, which always made my birthday seem extra special. Linda and Marcia, my two best friends, were there. I had a birthday cake and some presents, but I was expecting something more.

My mother said, "There's a present waiting for you in the barn, Holly." And I knew. I knew, I knew, I knew.

I took off running.

I was sure I could not hide my feelings completely as I stood staring at my big present. It was what it was and could never be anything else. Finally, I heard myself say, "Gee!" and then I said, "Wow!"

"Give her a try," my dad said.

I stepped forward and touched the smooth leather seat. **Columbia** was written in bold, bright letters on the red crossbar.

This was my first very own bike, but I already knew how to ride a two-wheeler. I threw my leg over and stood up on the pedal . . .

And I flew down Middlebury Road, pumping with all my might. I flew!

"I'll call you Beauty," I shouted into the rushing air. "Holly's Beauty."